The legend of King Arthur has come down to us out of the dim mists of history. All we know for certain is that when the Romans left Britain a warrior chief led a band of brave followers against the Saxon invaders. Around his heroic deeds grew the legend of Arthur and Excalibur, of Merlin and the Knights of the Round Table.

Like all good legends it has grown with the telling and who is to say that so brave a company would not also have found time to undertake adventurous deeds on behalf of the weak, the poor and the oppressed?

These are some of the stories from the legend. They may not have happened at all—but we can hope they did.

A certain amount of artist's licence has been found necessary in preparing the illustrations, in view of the lack of precise information about the period.

The deeds of the
nameless
knight

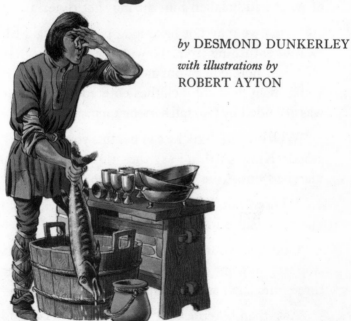

by DESMOND DUNKERLEY

with illustrations by
ROBERT AYTON

Ladybird Books Ltd Loughborough 1977

THE KNIGHT OF THE KITCHEN

"We shall not start our feast until some new wonder or adventure is brought to us," King Arthur announced.

A year had passed since the Fellowship of the Round Table had been formed. Now the knights were gathered again at Camelot and each had told of what had befallen him during that time.

"Then we may not have long to wait," said Sir Gawaine, turning from the window. "Unless I am mistaken here comes our new adventure now." A young man in shabby clothes entered the hall. He was attended by two tall serving men.

"Who do you think he can be, this young giant?" asked King Arthur as the three newcomers marched down the hall towards the king.

"I know not," answered Sir Gawaine, "but I like his looks, and he carries himself nobly."

"God save your majesty," said the young man, stopping in front of the king. "I have come to beg three gifts such as a king may easily give."

"Ask then," replied Arthur kindly. "Ask and you shall have them," for he, too, liked the honest look of the tall stranger.

"I ask now only that I may be allowed to eat, drink and lodge at your court for one year."

"A gift easily and willingly given," said the king, amazed at the simplicity of the request. "But is there nothing else?"

"Not until a year has passed, sire," replied the stranger. "Then will I ask for my other favours."

"Then may we not at least know your name, and where you come from?" enquired King Arthur.

"That too I may not say at present," was the reply.

Then King Arthur called Sir Kay, who was in charge of the royal household, and ordered that

the stranger be looked after as if he were a lord's son.

"Which he is not!" sneered Sir Kay later to Sir Lancelot, Sir Gawaine, Sir Gaheris and others. "He is more likely just an ordinary idler looking for a soft life at court. Well, I shall see that he doesn't get it, for he shall eat, sleep and work in the kitchen. And since he will not name himself I shall do it for him. I shall call him Beaumains – Fair Hands – for did you not see how white and soft they were?"

Both Sir Lancelot and Sir Gawaine reproached Sir Kay for his unkindness. "Beware of him," warned Sir Lancelot finally, "for he may yet surprise us all."

So for a whole year Beaumains, as he came to be known to everyone, worked in the kitchens. All that he was ordered to do he did quietly and cheerfully, even though Sir Kay never missed an opportunity to laugh at him, make jokes about him and say unkind things to him. Yet Beaumains never answered back and never lost his temper.

The other kitchen boys teased him at first, too, but soon grew to like him. Beaumains always won their wrestling and quarterstaff contests because of his size and great strength, but he never won unfairly and always with a smile and a kind word afterwards. Beaumains was a keen spectator, too, at the tournaments that were often held, and could be seen watching eagerly as the knights jousted.

9

So the year passed, Pentecost came once more, and the Fellowship of the Round Table had again gathered at Camelot.

"The reports I have heard are good," said King Arthur. "The borders of our kingdom are secure and our shores are free of Saxons. We have heard also of many good and knightly deeds. So now, as is our custom, we will delay our feast until some new happening or adventure presents itself."

At that moment the great doors at the far end of the hall swung open and a richly dressed young maiden approached the king's seat.

"I come to beg for help, my lord!" she cried, as she knelt in front of King Arthur.

"Who are you, and for whom do you seek help?" asked the king.

"I am the Lady Linnet," said the maiden, "and I seek assistance for my sister, the Lady Lyonesse. She is held captive in her castle by the Knight of the Red Lands, who has already slain many of your knights who have tried to rescue her."

The king's eyes flashed at this news and he looked angrily round at his knights. Before he could speak, however, a voice rang out clearly from the far end of the hall.

"My lord! May I thank you now for the twelve months' hospitality I have received at your court?" All eyes turned to Beaumains as he stepped forward from among the serving men. The angry king was about to wave him away impatiently when the young man said, "The other two gifts, sire! I ask now for the other two gifts you granted me."

"Speak then," said King Arthur, remembering his promise of a year ago.

"Firstly then, my lord, I ask your permission to assist this lady in her adventure," said Beaumains.

At this the maiden moved quickly away from Beaumains in disgust, for he looked and smelled of the kitchen. He was unaware of her scorn, however, as he continued to speak. "Secondly, sire, may Sir Lancelot of the Lake ride with me and make me a knight in your name when he considers that I am worthy of that honour?"

King Arthur looked across at Sir Lancelot, who rose from his seat, saying, "That will I gladly do."

"Then I, too, grant both your wishes and . . ." began the king, but the Lady Linnet interrupted him angrily.

"What insult and shame is this, my lord? I come to you, who have at your command the best knights in the world – Sir Lancelot, Sir Bedivere, Sir Bors and many others that are known throughout the land – and you would send me with a low born kitchen boy to save my lady sister!" In a great rage she swept from the hall.

Even as she left, the two attendants who had accompanied Beaumains when he first arrived and who had also spent the year in the kitchens, entered bearing armour and a huge sword which no one recognised.

"Where did he get those?" whispered Sir Bors to Sir Bedivere.

"Not in the kitchen, that's certain," replied Sir Bedivere, "and see, too, the fine horse that awaits him."

As all there wondered at these things, Beaumains mounted and rode away, followed shortly afterwards by Sir Lancelot.

When they had gone Sir Kay sprang to his feet. "The lady spoke truly!" he cried. "It is shame indeed! I will ride after this Knight of the Kitchen and put him in his place."

"Have a care then," called Sir Gawaine as Sir Kay stormed out of the hall, "for you may find more than you seek."

But Sir Kay took no notice and rode away, fully armed. He soon overtook Beaumains who was, by now, riding beside the maiden.

"Hey! Kitchen boy!" called Sir Kay. "Do you not know me?"

"I know you well," replied Beaumains, turning in his saddle. "I know you for the unkindest knight in all King Arthur's court."

Sir Kay immediately levelled his lance and rode furiously at Beaumains, expecting an easy victory. But the young man turned his horse aside at the last moment and knocked Sir Kay clean out of the saddle with a flat sweep of his sword. Then, dismounting, he took up his opponent's spear and shield, for he had neither of his own.

"Nobly done!" called Sir Lancelot who rode up at that moment. He had seen all that had happened and was amazed at the skill Beaumains had shown.

"I thank you, my lord," replied Beaumains, "but I know too little of these skills. Would you, sire, do me the honour of fighting with me so that I may learn from the finest in the land?"

"That will I!" replied Sir Lancelot with a laugh, and they both put their horses towards each other at a gallop. They met so fiercely that both were knocked out of their saddles. They leapt to their feet and the contest continued with sword and shield. They fought for more than an hour and Sir Lancelot was again amazed at his opponent's skill and strength. At length he lowered his sword. "Enough, Beaumains! Enough!" he cried breathlessly. "I can teach you nothing and am only glad that we fight as friends."

"And I," replied Beaumains with a laugh, as he, too, lowered his sword point. Then he stood before Sir Lancelot.

"Will you now, my lord, grant the king's third favour, and make me a knight?"

"That I would do gladly," replied Sir Lancelot, "but first I must know your name and where you come from."

Beaumains stood silent for a moment. "In secrecy only then, my lord, and tell no one?" he asked. Sir Lancelot gave his word and Beaumains spoke softly in the other's ear.

"Ah!" exclaimed Sir Lancelot, stepping back a pace and grasping the young man's hand, "I knew

it would be something like this. Now will I gladly
knight you.''

So Beaumains knelt before Sir Lancelot, who
touched him lightly on the shoulder and named
him knight.

"Farewell now, and good fortune go with you,"
said Sir Lancelot. "Depart on your adventure,
while I return to Camelot with Sir Kay who seems
in no condition to ride alone." With a wave of his
hand Sir Lancelot turned and set off back to
Camelot, while Beaumains rode off after the Lady
Linnet.

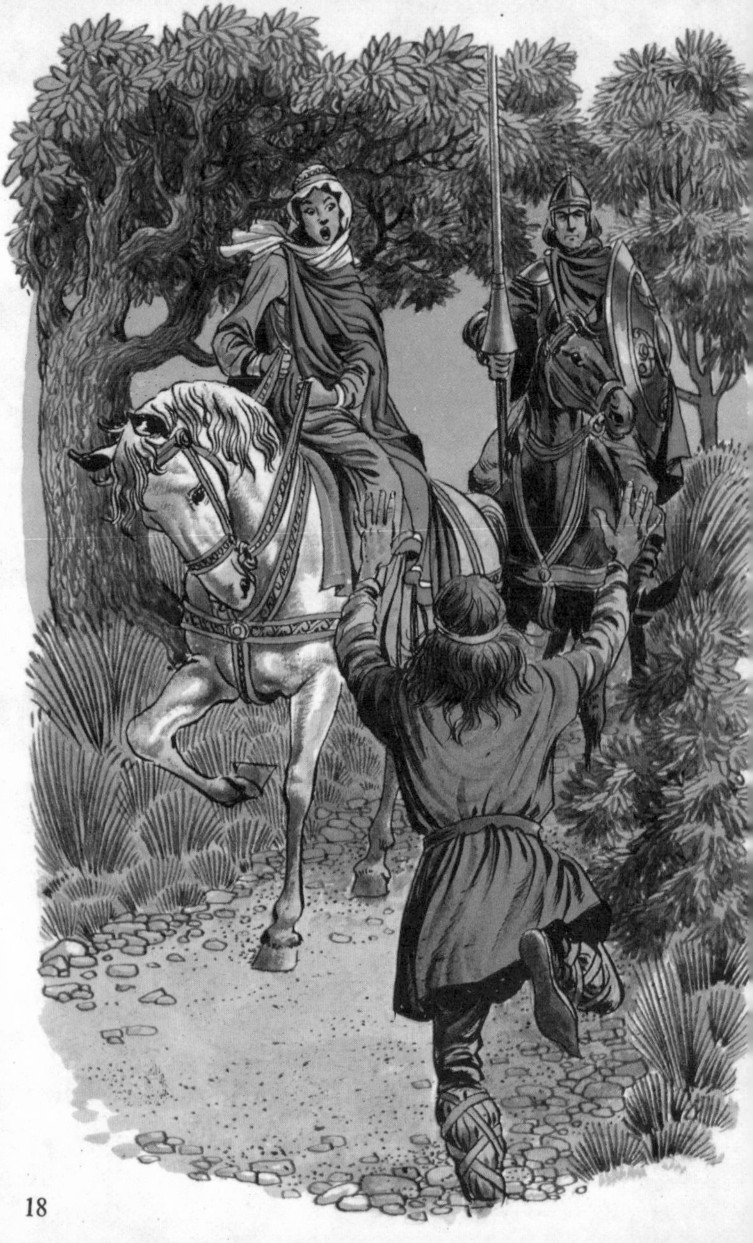

THE BLACK KNIGHT AND THE GREEN

"What are you doing here?" cried Linnet rudely as Beaumains rode up. "I know you now by the foul smell of your clothes. You are the kitchen boy they called Beaumains. Do you really think that such as you can help my sister? Get back to your cooking!"

"Lady," answered Beaumains politely, "you can say what you will to me but I will never turn back."

"Then may you be sorry for it," replied Linnet unkindly, "for we go to meet those who will surely kill you."

"Be that as it may," was the quiet reply. "King Arthur has trusted me with your adventure, and if I must die for it, then die I will."

These brave words made no difference to the maiden, and they rode on in silence, the Lady Linnet always a little way ahead.

In a while they came to a small wood. As they were about to ride through it, a man came running from the trees. "Turn back, sir, turn back!" he shouted. "Take not the lady through the wood for there are robbers there and they are attacking my lord."

"Show me!" cried Beaumains, drawing his sword and spurring his horse forward. The squire ran with him, holding the stirrup leather. As they burst into a clearing in the trees three men ran out at them. The two in front were immediately cut down. The third, turning to run, fell under the hooves of Beaumain's horse. On the far side of the clearing three more men were busily tying a knight to a tree. They turned in terror and ran off into the trees pursued by Beaumains, while the squire went to the aid of his master.

"I owe you my life, sir," said the knight when Beaumains returned. "Come with me to my castle which is nearby so that I may reward you."

"I need no payment for such a duty," replied Beaumains.

"Then at least stay to eat and sleep, for it is almost dark."

When they reached the castle, however, Linnet refused to sit at the same table as Beaumains. "He is only a cook's boy from King Arthur's kitchen," she said scornfully. "It is not fit that I should sit with him." So Beaumains and the knight sat talking and laughing at one table while Linnet sat alone and in silence at another.

"You had best begone, Sir Kitchen Knight," said Linnet next morning after they had been riding for about two hours. "Begone while there is still time, for yonder is the tent of the Black Knight of the Thorn. He is the greatest fighter in all this part of the land and he will surely kill you."

They had stopped at the edge of a wide, shallow stream and following her gaze Beaumains saw a strange sight. Beneath a blackthorn tree was pitched a tent of black silk. A black shield hung from a tent pole and upright in the ground beside it was stuck a black spear. A knight in black armour sat on a stone beneath the tree and he looked up as they approached.

"Is this your champion from King Arthur's court?" the Black Knight called across the water.

"Heaven forbid!" replied Linnet. "He is only a boy from King Arthur's kitchen who follows me against my will."

"Why then I cannot fight him, since he is no knight," called back the Black Knight, rising from his seat and mounting his horse which was standing nearby. "But at least I'll teach him a lesson. I'll take his horse and armour and he can walk back to Camelot!" With a roar of laughter the Black Knight pulled his spear from the ground and spurred his great horse into the water. Beaumains set his horse forward to meet him crying, "Take them if you can!"

The two met in mid-stream amid a shower of spray set up by the horses' hooves. The Black Knight's spear shattered to pieces on his opponent's shield. Beaumains' lance, however, glanced off the shield of the Black Knight and pierced his side. Though badly wounded the Black Knight tried to draw his sword, but the effort was too much for him and he fell dead from his horse.

"That was a cowardly blow," cried Linnet. "He said he would not fight and yet you struck him down," and with that she rode quickly away. Beaumains did not answer but got down from his horse and put on the fallen knight's armour, for he could see that it was better than his own. Then

mounting the Black Knight's horse he rode off after the Lady Linnet.

As he caught up with her he was again greeted with unkind words.

"Away, kitchen knight, where I cannot smell you," she jeered. "What shame that such a knight as that should be killed by a coward's blow."

"I am no coward, lady, as well you know," answered Beaumains quietly.

"That you will have to prove now, or fly for your life," said Linnet suddenly, reining in her horse. Riding towards them was a knight in green armour, carrying a green shield and spear.

"Greetings, lady," called the Green Knight. "Is that my brother, the Black Knight of the Thorn, who rides with you?"

"No, sir knight," replied Linnet. "It is but a kitchen boy from Camelot who has just now killed your brother with a coward's blow."

"Then he shall die for it!" cried the Green Knight in a rage. At the first clash both lances broke and the Green Knight was driven from the saddle. Swiftly he leapt to his feet, drawing his sword. Beaumains, too, dismounted and they rushed at each other, cutting and hacking.

"Shame on you, sir knight!" called Linnet when they had been fighting furiously for nearly an hour. "Why do you take so long to teach a kitchen boy a lesson?"

The Green Knight became so angry at these words that he rushed forward swinging his sword wildly. Beaumains avoided his charge and gave him such a blow that he fell to the ground. Beaumains stood over the Green Knight with sword upraised.

"Mercy, I beg you!" pleaded the fallen knight.

"No mercy," replied Beaumains, "unless this lady herself begs for it."

"That I will never do," cried Linnet. "I will never beg from a mere kitchen boy."

"Then he shall die," said Beaumains grimly.

"Spare me," pleaded the Green Knight. "Spare me and I and fifty of my knights will serve you while we live."

"That matters not. The lady here must ask for your life," repeated Beaumains.

"Never!" said Linnet again. "It would shame me too much to ask you for anything." So Beaumains raised his sword to strike but as he did so the Lady Linnet stepped quickly forward. "Do not kill him, you cowardly wretch! Put down your sword."

"Lady," said Beaumains politely, "your request is always my command." He lowered his sword and allowed the Green Knight to stand up. "Sir Green Knight of the Wood, I spare your life at the request of this lady."

In gratitude the Green Knight took Beaumains and the lady to his castle where a feast was prepared. As before Linnet refused to sit at the same table as Beaumains, although he was treated with great honour by everyone else.

Next morning the Green Knight rode with them some distance on their way. When it was time for

them to go on alone the Green Knight told
Beaumains that he and his fifty knights would be
ready to serve him whenever they were required.

"Ride with them to Camelot then," commanded
Beaumains. "Tell King Arthur why you have
come and that the Knight of the Kitchen sent you.
The service you owe is not to me but to the king
whose knight I am."

THE BLUE KNIGHT AND THE RED

The Lady Linnet had not stayed to hear this but had ridden on ahead. Now she sat still on her horse at the crest of a small hill.

"Are you ready to fly for your life now, sir kitchen knight?" she asked, looking at the scene below. "For see, there is the castle of the Knight of the Blue Water. Only Sir Lancelot, Sir Bedivere or King Arthur himself could hope to defeat him in battle, so you surely have no chance."

Beaumains looked at the white castle set beside the blue waters of a lake.

"He must be a great knight indeed," he replied calmly, "and one that I look forward to meeting."

"You will meet him soon enough, you fool," cried Linnet, "and his anger will be great when he hears that you have killed one of his brothers and defeated the other. What is more, he has a following of one hundred knights, so now you will surely be put in your place."

"If he is as great a knight as you say," laughed Beaumains, "then he will not send all of his one hundred knights against me at the same time. And if he sends them one at a time I will do my best with each until my strength gives out. No man can do more than that whether he come from court or kitchen."

When she heard these brave words the lady began to feel sorry for the way she had treated Beaumains. She remembered all the unkind things she had said to this brave and unknown young man, and her heart was sad.

"Sir," she said in a gentler voice, "you speak bravely, and I know in my heart that you have acted bravely. But even so I beg you to turn back now before it is too late. You and your horse are tired after three days' travelling and fighting, and I am sure that you will get hurt or killed now if you go on."

"That I cannot do, my lady," said Beaumains, surprised at the first kind words she had ever spoken to him, "though I thank you for the kind thought. Besides it would be a shame to turn back now when we are so close to rescuing your sister."

Linnet tried again to change his mind. "But sir, I plead with you to do so. The strength of this Blue Knight, even if you defeat him, is nothing compared to that of the Knight of the Red Lands whom you will then have to meet before my sister is rescued. Strong as you are I feel you can have little hope against him."

"Nevertheless, I must try, lady, for it is my duty."

"You make me feel ashamed," replied Linnet quietly, for she was close to tears. "It must be that you come from some great and noble family," she continued, "for I have always treated you with scorn yet you have never once lost your temper.

I have spoken nothing but unkind words to you yet you have never once answered me harshly."

"As to that," replied Beaumains, "your unkind words have helped me, for they made me feel so angry that they gave more strength to my blows and helped me to defeat your enemies. As to who I am and where I come from, you will know that only when your sister is freed and I have finished the adventure granted me by the king."

Linnet started to speak again but Beaumains stopped her. "All I will tell you now," he said, "is that I have not spent all my life in the kitchen at Camelot and whether I am knight or kitchen boy I have done you knight's service."

"That is true, Sir Beaumains," said Linnet softly and with great kindness, "and I ask you now to forgive me for the way I have treated you and spoken to you."

"With all my heart," cried Beaumains, "and there is now no knight in the whole world I would not fight for the sake of yourself or your sister."

"Then God be with you," she said quickly, "for see, the Blue Knight has seen us and sends a squire."

"My lord asks whether you come in peace or war?" demanded the messenger.

"In peace if he will let us pass," replied Beaumains, "otherwise it must be war."

The Blue Knight, mounted on a great grey horse, came thundering from the gate towards them. Beaumains also set his horse down the hill at great speed. The two knights met with such force that both horses and riders were hurled to the ground. The knights leapt to their feet and set

on each other furiously. For two hours the fight raged until their armour was dented and their shields battered.

Beaumains finally managed a blow of such strength that the Blue Knight fell and lay still. Instantly Beaumains leapt to stand over him with sword raised. Linnet, who had watched the fight, ran quickly forward and put her hand on Beaumains' sword arm. "Spare his life for my sake," she said gently.

"Willingly," cried Beaumains, helping the fallen knight to his feet. "He has fought well, and does not deserve to die."

"I thank you for my life," said the Blue Knight breathlessly, "for now I know that you are the same strong knight who killed my brothers, the Black Knight of the Thorn and the Green Knight of the Wood."

"I am," replied Beaumains, "but the Green Knight lives and is even now on his way to Camelot with fifty knights to serve King Arthur."

"Then tomorrow I will join him with my one hundred knights," said the Blue Knight joyfully. "But first you and the fair lady must rest in my castle."

That night at supper the Lady Linnet asked Beaumains if she could sit with him, and the three feasted merrily together.

"Tell me, lady," said the Blue Knight as they were sitting at their ease after the meal, "where are you leading this brave knight whose name I know not?"

"Sir," replied Linnet sadly, "he is going to free my sister who is held prisoner by the Knight of the Red Lands."

"Then it is a dangerous adventure indeed," said the Blue Knight urgently, "for it is said that this knight of whom you speak has the strength of ten men and is the most dangerous knight in the world." He turned to Beaumains. "He has killed many knights who have tried to rescue the fair lady, but still he keeps her prisoner hoping that Sir Lancelot or even King Arthur himself will attempt the rescue, for he hates all true knights but those two most of all."

Beaumains and Linnet continued their journey in silence next morning for both were thinking of the Blue Knight's words. They had been riding for some three hours when their horses shied suddenly and started back in fear.

"What is this?" exclaimed Beaumains in horror, for hanging from the trees nearby were the bodies of many knights, with their shields and swords hung beside them.

"They are the dead knights who have already attempted what you are about to try," answered Linnet sadly.

"This is a most shameful thing," said Beaumains quietly but with great anger. "This evil knight well deserves to die. Come, let us hurry!"

A little further on the trees ended and a broad grassy plain stretched out before them. Away on the far side stood a castle of red rock surrounded by the tents of the Red Knight's followers. Beaumains would have spurred his horse forward at once so eager was he to avenge the deaths of those dead knights, but Linnet stopped him.

"Sir," she said, "those who wish to challenge the Red Knight must first blow the horn that hangs there on the last tree. But do not act too hastily," she went on quickly, catching at Beaumains' arm that was already reaching out for the horn. "It is said that the Red Knight's strength is at its greatest before the hour of noon. Then it gets less and less until by evening he is no stronger than other men."

Beaumains shook his arm free. "No!" he said fiercely. "No, I will fight him now, strong as he is, or die in the attempt." With that he seized the horn and blew so long and loud a blast that knights came running from the tents, and people crowded to the walls and windows of the castle.

Then Beaumains saw a tall man running from the largest tent, buckling on his sword as he ran. He was dressed all in red armour, and as he ran a red shield and spear were handed to him. Then he rode his war horse to a long clearing beside the tents and waited until Beaumains approached.

"There is your enemy, sir," said Linnet fearfully. "And there at the window is my sister."

Beaumains followed Linnet's pointing finger and saw, looking from a high window, the loveliest face he had ever seen. His heart went out to her at once and he said, "She is truly the fairest lady I have ever seen, and makes the danger I face now seem nothing."

"Why do you look so long at my lady?" called the rough voice of the Red Knight. "Look to me, for your body will soon be hanging with those others."

"She is not your lady," replied Beaumains sternly. "It is to free her from you, and to avenge those dead knights, that I come now to kill you."

The Red Knight laughed scornfully. "Another boastful fool from Arthur's Round Table. Tell me your name, Sir Black Knight, that I may know who it is I am to hang."

"My name matters not to you," said Beaumains, "and I am not yet a member of King Arthur's noble Fellowship of the Round Table. Only when I have rid the world of such an evil knight as you will I ask the king for that honour!"

"That's talk enough!" shouted the Knight of the Red Lands, and set his horse towards Beaumains at a great gallop. So great was the crash when they met that both horses fell dead and the riders lay stunned. They soon recovered and dashed at each other with their swords, hacking and cutting so furiously that pieces flew off their armour and their shields became useless.

Beaumains soon realised that the Red Knight was by far the strongest and fiercest opponent he had yet met. The blows he struck ceaselessly upon Beaumains were as powerful as even those of Sir Lancelot, and often had the young man reeling. But thoughts of the beautiful face he had seen at the window, and of the dead knights hanging on the trees, gave Beaumains extra strength and soon the Red Knight was staggering also.

They fought long into the afternoon until both could scarcely stand. Then, weak with weariness, Beaumains heard Linnet's voice.

"Oh, my poor sister. She weeps and cries, for she is sure that you too are beaten and she must stay a prisoner."

Beaumains looked quickly up at the window and saw the Lady Lyonesse sobbing with her head in her hands. The sight gave him the strength for one last great blow, which crashed the Red Knight to the ground. With a cry of triumph Beaumains stood astride him and cut the fastenings of his helmet. Then the Red Knight cried for mercy.

"Coward and shameful knight," said Beaumains, "you deserve only such pity as you gave others." With that he killed him with a great sweep of his sword. Then Beaumains fell to the ground beside him, unconscious from the many wounds he had received.

"Where am I?" he asked weakly when he awoke.

"In the tent of the Red Knight," answered the Lady Linnet from close by. "You have lain here for a whole week so still that at times my sister feared you dead."

"Then I must go to her," said Beaumains. He stood up slowly and with difficulty, armed himself and rode to the castle gate.

There he found the drawbridge was up. As he waited, a voice called down from the battlements.

"Sir, I am Sir Gringamor, brother to the Lady Lyonesse. I know well that you are a brave fighter, but you may not see my sister until I know who you are and of what family."

Beaumains was about to answer angrily when a trumpet sounded behind them. Turning, Beaumains saw a company of knights riding across the plain towards them, flying King Arthur's pennant. The leading knight rode straight up to Beaumains crying, "Gareth! Gareth, my brother, you tricked us all!"

Then Beaumains clasped the other's hand, for this was his own brother, Sir Gaheris, sent by King Arthur to bring him back safely to Camelot.

Sir Gringamor had lowered the drawbridge and the company clattered into the courtyard.

"Sir Knight," said Sir Gringamor, "tell me who is this brave knight who will not tell his name?"

"He is Sir Gareth, youngest son of the King of

Orkney. He is also my brother, and brother to Sir Gawaine," answered Sir Gaheris. "We did not know him when he came to court for he was only a child when we left home. Then messengers arrived in Camelot from my father inquiring after him. Only then did we realise that the unknown knight, the fame of whose deeds had reached court by the knights he defeated and sent there, must be our brother Gareth!"

"I thank you, sir," said Sir Gringamor, and taking Sir Gareth by the hand he led him to where the Lady Lyonesse was waiting.

Later, at the court of King Arthur in Camelot, they were married amid much feasting and rejoicing.

Sir Gareth, now a member of the Fellowship of the Round Table, became one of King Arthur's foremost knights. He took part in many more dangerous adventures and performed many valiant deeds, but none brought him more fame than the first when he was simply Beaumains, the Knight of the Kitchen.